Emily Car

by
Professer Clickity Klunk

Illustrated by
Gerald W. Tisdale

Published by

**DOWN THE PATH
PUBLISHING**

First Edition

Published in Canada 2010
by Down the Path Publishing
PO Box 344, Clearwater B.C. V0E 1N0
Printed in China
e-mail:books@ProfesserKlunk.com
David@DownThePathPublishing.com

Library and Archives Canada Cataloguing in Publication
Klunk, Clickity, 1955-
Emily Car / by Professer Klunk; illustrations by Gerald W. Tisdale.

(A cautionary tale by Professer Klunk)
Also issued in mini softcover format.

ISBN 978-0-9865417-3-5

I. Tisdale, Gerald W II. Title
III. Series:°Klunk, Clickity, 1955- . Cautionary tale.

PS8621.L856E45 2010 jC811'.6 C2010-902865-1

Emily Car

Now this is a story

About Emily Car;

She drove into a field

Where she drove pretty far.

This field was quite soft

It was actually muck.

Emily sank in and

Now she was stuck.

Just then Tommy arrived

In his four wheel drive

Said, "I'll pull you out

Then we can go for a ride."

Tommy drove in,

Tied a rope to his truck,

Stepped down on the gas,

Sank in and was stuck.

Farmer Brown's tractor

Was ploughing that day,

Saw Emily and Tommy

And this he did say.

"I have a chain

I will hook on to you,"

Then Farmer Brown's tractor

Sank down in the goo.

Eddie the excavator
On his caterpillar track,
Hooked on with his shovel
Blew smoke out his stack.

His treads grabbed the grass

Tossed up clumps with a spin;

Eddie inched forward,

Then he sank in.

Sammy the steamroller

Said "I'll flatten it down"

Rolled onto the field

Then sank into the ground.

Emily yelled "Hey!

I know what to do;

If we all go quickly forward

We can get free of this goo."

Their engines all roared

And daylight went dim;

The air filled with muck

As the wheels did spin.

Do you know what happened?

The guck came down with a schmuck

Then, everyone except Emily

Became covered in muck.

Tommy cried "Hey!

Emily is still clean;

Let's all go in reverse"

The engines did scream.

Again lots of mud

Flew up in the sky;

When it all landed

Not a windscreen was dry.

Back then forth, back and forth

Together they hove;

Then suddenly forward slowly

Out they all drove.

Sometimes back and forth

Are the moves one should make;

When wishing to resolve

A sticky mistake.

About the Artist

Gerald W. Tisdale
Cartoonist.

Now living in Clearwater B.C.
Gerald is the creator of
"TisToons" cartoons which
have been published in
numerous papers through out
British Columbia over the
past twenty years, and

Photo by Sherry Tisdale

are currently published in the Clearwater Times on a
regular basis. He was nominated to one of the three
finalists for cartoon category in the British Columbia and
Yukon Community Newspaper Association 2010 Ma Murray
Awards.

Proofread by Helen Moller

Other Books by Professer Clickity Klunk

A Puppy Named Rufus & Mini
Horace the Cat & Mini
Wishfilled Thinking & Mini
Whoa There Now Nelly & Mini
Her Beef Stew & Mini
Emily Car Mini

**DOWN THE PATH
PUBLISHING**

www.ProfesserKlunk.com